P9-DZX-663

Copyright © 2002 by Coppenrath Verlag, 48155 Münster, Germany.

First published in Germany under the title *Hasenmatz will fliegen*

English translation copyright © 2004 by Parklane Publishing. All rights reserved.

First published in the United States and Canada in 2004 by Parklane Publishing,

a division of Book Club of America Inc., Hauppauge, New York.

This edition was prepared by Cheshire Studio.

ISBN1-59384-042-X / Printed in China

1 3 5 7 9 10 8 6 4 2

Benjamin Bunny Learns to Fly

Rolf Fänger & Ulrike Möltgen

Translated by Marianne Martens

PARKLANE PUBLISHING · HAUPPAUGE, NEW YORK

Once there was a little rabbit named Benjamin Bunny who climbed to the top of a very tall hill. As he looked down over the meadow and the forest he thought to himself, "Wouldn't it be great if I could fly like my friend Red Bird?"

He told his friend Bella Bunny about his idea.

Bella looked at him sternly. "Now, Benjamin," she said, "this is just another one of your crazy ideas. You know that rabbits can't fly!"

"I think it would be fun to try!" he exclaimed, and he ran off to talk to his friend Butterfly about flying.

"What a good idea," said Butterfly. "I'd love it if you could fly. We'd have so much fun. I'll teach you. Copy what I do."

Butterfly flapped his wings up and down, and Benjamin Bunny did the same thing with his arms. He hopped up in the air—but BANG! He crashed to the ground.

"Oops-a-daisy!" said Butterfly. "Are you hurt?"

"No, no, I'm okay," said Benjamin Bunny. "I'll bet Red Bird
fell down a few times, too, when he was learning how to fly."

"I'm sure you're right," said Butterfly. "You did well for a beginner.
Why don't you go talk to Bee? Maybe she can help."

"Well," said Bee, "the problem is obvious. Just look at your pants! You'll never fly with pants striped like that. They're all wrong. The stripes need to be like mine. And don't forget to buzz like I do. Buzzing is very important."

"Thanks for the tip," said Benjamin Bunny. "I didn't know that."
"But where can we get stripes?" asked Froggie, who also wanted to try flying. Benjamin Bunny knew just where to go. Soon they were striped just like bees, and they ran off, buzzing, into the field.

"What on earth are you doing?" asked Ladybug, as Benjamin Bunny and Froggie buzzed madly around the field.

"We're practicing our flying!" they shouted. "It isn't working yet!"

"Let me have a look at your wings," said Ladybug.

They held their arms high and Ladybug spotted the problem immediately. "They're too thin," she said, "and the color is wrong."

"Oh, well," said Froggie. "I was really looking forward to flying. But maybe we're just not meant to fly. Come on, Benjamin, let's go swimming instead. I'll teach you— it's easy! Take a deep breath and move your arms back and forth in front of you like this."

"These aren't arms," said Benjamin Bunny. "They're my wings! And I don't want to learn to swim. I want to learn to fly—just like Red Bird. I've already figured out how to make wings that look just like Ladybug's. Why don't you come back here and help me?"

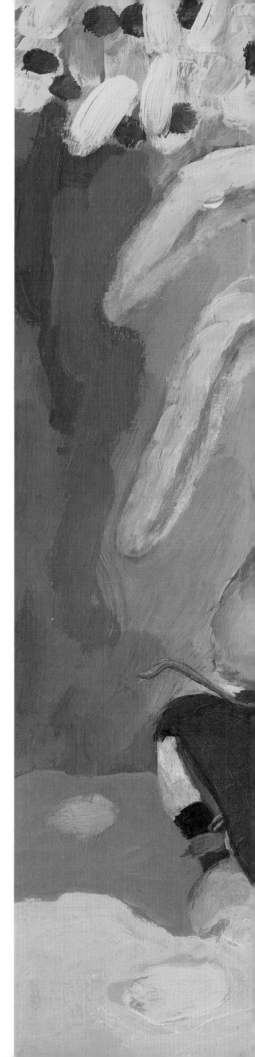

When the ladybug wings were finished, Benjamin decided to visit Sylvia Hen to ask if she had any advice about flying.

"Let's see," she clucked. "If you're going to fly, you'll need a nice beak like mine. You can always tell a real flyer by his beak. Just look at your friend Red Bird. He has a big, yellow beak, and I've heard that he can fly all the way to Africa!"

"Well," said Benjamin Bunny, "I guess I'll just have to make a nice beak. With my bee stripes, ladybug wings, and chicken beak, I'll be able to fly to Africa, too!"

"Look what I found!" called Froggie, as Benjamin Bunny tried on his new beak. He held out three big beautiful feathers, tied together with string. "Red Bird has feathers, so you probably need some, too."

"Are you sure you don't want them?" asked Benjamin Bunny.

"No, thanks," said Froggie. "I think I'd rather swim than fly. Just make sure you wave to me when you're way up high in the air."

At last, Benjamin Bunny was ready for his first flight. All his friends came out to the field to watch.

"Nice stripes," said Bee.

"The beak looks perfect!" said Sylvia Hen.

"Such beautiful wings," said Ladybug proudly.

"Don't forget the feathers," said Froggie. "All birds have feathers."

Suddenly, a big shadow moved across the meadow.

It was Red Bird!

"Well, well!" he said as he fluttered to the ground. "I see there's a new bird in the neighborhood. What's your name?"

"Umm . . . I'm Jet Bird!" stuttered Benjamin.

"Jet Bird? You don't look like any bird I've ever seen. Let's fly together and see who can go the highest."

"Tomorrow," said Benjamin. "Tomorrow would be better."

"No, no, no," said Red Bird. "*Right now*. On your mark, get set, go!"

"WAIT!" shouted Bella Bunny. "Our friend Jet Bird is accustomed to taking a running start. Run over to those three trees and take off from there."

Red Bird peered off across the field. "All the way over there? I'm not very good at running, but if you insist."

"On your mark, get set, go!" shouted all the friends at once.

The two birds started to run. At first Red Bird was able to keep up, but soon he started to huff and puff, and Benjamin—being a rabbit, of course—bounded past him.

Just as Benjamin reached the top of the hill he jumped up as far as he could, spread his wings widely, and a big gust of wind lifted him right into the air.

He was flying!

Down below, his friends waved and cheered and Red Bird lay exhausted against a rock.

Benjamin soared higher and higher. He could see everything for miles around. Flying was more wonderful than he had ever imagined.

But suddenly the wind died down and Benjamin started to tumble to the ground!

Luckily, he landed with a big splash in the middle of Froggie's pond. Luckier still, he remembered what Froggie had said about swimming so he managed to make it to shore.

"You're an amazing rabbit!" exclaimed Red Bird. "First you fly like a bird, then you swim like a frog!"

"Thank you," said Benjamin proudly, "but I couldn't have done it without the help of my best friends."

"I'm getting ready to fly off to Africa again," said Red Bird. "Want to come along?"

"No, thanks," said Benjamin Bunny. "Flying is fun, but there are lots of other things I want to learn how to do!"